I0822829

SLAVE ME NO MORE

SLAVE ME NO MORE

ATALAYA SHORTRIDGE

Shortridge Books

First Printing, 2024

CHAPTER 1

Chapter 1

"'Aight, boys! You gotta git workin'!" The overseer demanded of his prisoners. The slaves worked dawn to dusk, shoveling the dirt or tilling the soil beneath their bare feet. It was a poor life, barely surviving. But they did survive, at least. The men were tortured. So were the women. Having to constantly babysit the kids, feed the kids, nurture the kids, kids, kids, kids, and some women even worked with the men. Also, all slaves were separated from their family. 'Aw, you got a family picture? *Rip!*' Barely any wives were with husbands, or children with mothers or fathers!

"Boys!! Stop slowin' down!!" The overseer then whipped Charlie at an excruciating point, and overruling the "ooh..."s. Charlie was only a child, so it hurt so much more than average. Charlie fell in the mud, a fifth of his clothing sets, gone. They only had so much clothes.

"Get up, Char', you're not dead!" The overseer blasted in Charlie's ear. He got back on his feet immediately and started to continue picking wheat. Amelia rushed over to help him. She had slight mud on her face and wheat fluffs all over, soil everywhere on her feet, but a bright smile. Amelia was a very kind child.

"Oh, Charlie, you okay? You don't look so good." She said, every now and then pausing due to her ignorance of English. It was illegal to teach them English. In the middle of brushing the dirt off him, the overhead spotted her out of line.

"YOU!!" The overseer screamed at her from a distance. Overseers had a huge edge over the black slaves, you couldn't scare them. You'd be scared half to death if they spotted you out of order. You could be killed.

"GET OVER HERE!" Walking as he screamed, the overseer continued.

"You get over here right now, get back in line in three seconds!!!"

Hurrying over, the overhead counted.

"One.."

Amelia ran over to her crops.

"Two.."

Amelia started to sprint, and almost made it when-

"THREE!!"

She was too late. Three rang

"Please- s-sir- d-don-n't k-kill me. Please, sir, please no- no-please- don't" She said scared and shaky as the overhead approached her.

"I counted to three, you didn't flee, so why don't I say bye? Let the owner decide if you die!" It was the poem that was a signal that you were sent to the owner, the cruel, injust, owner, who barely ever let the slaves live. Only two ever were allowed. One was Charlie.

The slaves gasped as Amelia was standing there, cornered, and dumbfounded.

"Y-yes, I know the address." Was the response that meant the slave was to go to the owner.

CHAPTER 2

Chapter 2

Charlie was partly a wimp of the slaves. Overseers picked on him. Just more excruciating of a life than the others, but he lived with it. Charlie had heard of a way out of slavery. A risky route that was riddled with slave hunters, a series of people helping the slaves, hiding them in a secret compartment, running down and helping them every now and then. It seemed amazing, but the risk. And he didn't know enough about it. He knew it also had something to do with trains.. It was all too confusing for him. He had also heard if you were caught by anyone other than the helpers, there was a chance you could be *killed.* Charlie shivered at the thought of it. A bullet going through him for getting a better life. Ah, he just knew he would at least get a bit of affection from Amelia. Risking her life for him... Oh, wait, did the overhead catch her? Wait, *where's Amelia?!*

Frantically searching, he saw the overseer, and remembered his job. Slavery. Amelia will take care of herself, right? He could only hope.

CHAPTER 3

Chapter 3

Amelia was now before the cruel owner. The owner definitely seemed like he was going to kill her. She kneeled before him, begging for mercy from their cruel owner. He could buy people, there wasn't a law against that! But look at all the other laws they've created that's going against them..

"Oh, please, master, I don't want to die! What would you do without your only woman on the field?"

"Your testimony is pathetic. I will kill you- bup-bup-bup- if.."

Amelia was scared of what he was going to continue with. Would she be crucified?

".. You keep being sympathetic. Get to work and don't you dare stop this time!"

A sigh of relief came from Amelia. The owner then literally threw her out, having her collapse on the floor, looking up at the door in despair.

Charlie realized she had fallen. He felt terribly for her. It was not right. Nobody should be in excruciating pain like the slaves are! They needed to stand up for the justice they didn't have. He wanted to do something. But he was just the wimp.

CHAPTER 4

Chapter 4

Amelia started to cry on the floor.

"Get up Amelia!!! You gonna lie there the entire day or you gonna git to work?!" The overseer blurted, the outcry shooting bits of saliva out on the poor Amelia. She had tears in her eyes, and went up to the overseer and said with her hands prepared for prayer, and a glisten in her eyes: "But, sir! You mustn't do this!"

"What you gon' do 'bout it?" The overseer screamed in her ears. Amelia nearly fell back at the sound.

Amelia got back to her plow. She sighed.

Charlie's blood was beginning to boil. He had heard the whole conversation. Hatred started to spread through his mind, like a contagious virus of hate. He got angrier, angrier, angrier until he was unable to resist. He swiftly spun round, a hundred and eighty degrees, to the overseer that was directly behind him. He said-

"YOU OUGHTN'T DO THIS!!!" At first, the slaves were confused, but then realized he was right. This would only stop if they stepped up.

"Yeah, this isn't right! We didn't ask to be black!!" One slave spit at the overhead from the top-left of the farm.

"We deserve the same rights!" Another slave got out of their shell and stood up.

"YEAH!" Another slave spit at the overhead, with the act of putting a fist in the air.

"We don't deserve this!!" Another step-up from the right team.

One slave after another, there became an army of voices and outcries standing up for what was right. Amelia was the only one who had not yet joined the fight.

"Amelia?" Charlie asked in the middle of the noise.

The overseer raised an eyebrow.

"People," Amelia said while signaling for silence (which she received) "This isn't right. The only way we get out of this is making sure that the overhead, and our master," Amelia continued while pointing her finger toward the owner's house. The owner poked his head through the window. The overseer mouthed "I don't know" to the owner before continuing to bite his fingernails.

"..get the message that we need a change!!" Amelia put her fist in the air. The slaves chanted the words: "We want change! You hear? Change!!"

The crazy and amazing event was about to end when the owner came out.

"Hey! Stop the racket!!" The owner screamed. The owner was a lot scarier. They got quiet.

"WHO STARTED THIS?! Huh? Riddle me that!" There was an awkward silence. Charlie had a sigh of relief. They had his back. Suddenly they all pointed at Charlie. All except Amelia, who stood biting her fingernails.

The owner lunged up to Charlie, pointing a finger under his chin.

"You little! I'll-"

Suddenly Amelia stood up when they all were scared.

"This isn't right!! We started this rally for change! Must it stop now?!"

The slaves looked around. But suddenly one yelled in the silence: "NO!"

Another screamed: "NO!!"

One after another the fight was back, chanting and yelling: "No, no, no, no, no..." There was no stopping them. Until the owner shut up Charlie with a leaf to mouth and dragged him to the dungeon yelling: "This is what happens when you rebel against me. *You* mustn't do *this!*" Gasps and whispers commenced. There was no beating the owner. But a spirit stayed in Amelia. One last hope.

CHAPTER 5

Chapter 5

Meanwhile, after Charlie had left his cell, the Underground Railroad was being used by slaves all around. But hardly any of the slaves survived the way out, because the more slaves along the Underground Railroad, the more slave catchers hiding in plain sight, waiting for their prey. Amelia dreamed of the Underground Railroad, imagining it being her destiny. She was confident, yet weak. On the other hand, Charlie was strong, yet hesitant.

Amelia would convince Charlie. She would do it. No matter what. No matter if he says:

"No, absolutely not. You ought to go to the owner without permission instead of this. You'll get the same outcome. And also, I've already been arrested."

Charlie was very confident about his opinion. But Amelia pleaded while turning to face Charlie when he tried to ignore her and drink water for once.

"Oh, but Charlie, I am weak, you are strong. Very strong. So please, Charlie. I'll call you Charles." Charlie smiled. He liked being called Charles. He felt sophisticated and able. This was Charlie's only chance to get out of this.

"Alrighty, then. I'll- I'll go."

"Yes!" Amelia whispered to herself.

CHAPTER 6

Chapter 6

Panting, Jamie started to head towards her home. Her home was not only a home, it was a slave hotel. A slave catcher was running behind her. Somehow, the slave catcher found out that she is hiding slaves currently. She had a family of three. The child met their parents for the second time in their life.

But the slave catcher was there. Chasing her. Suddenly, after tears and multiple turns, she lost the slave catcher. Jamie got home, and signaled with a lamp to the slaves with Morse Code:

"I'm home. A slave catcher almost followed me. Be aware. Look out your window every now and then."

The slaves tried their best. They signaled:

"O-o 'scretch' 'dat'. Ok."

Jamie smiled. She hung up her coat and went down to the slaves.

"Alright, guys. Dinner will be in an hour. Jack, you mustn't do that when I let you outside, okay? People think it's rude. Pattie, I got the medicine you needed. Nathan, be careful on that leg, it's got a sore. And, oh, I'll give you your clothes to change into. Okay, that is it. Use Morse Code if you need anything."

Jamie took care of the slaves very well. But she was going to let them head to the free lands tomorrow.

CHAPTER 7

Chapter 7

The day Amelia and Charlie (mostly Amelia) planned to sneak out arrived. The fear from Charlie or Charles filled the room, while Amelia still enjoyed the anticipation. Charlie tried whatever was possible to convince Amelia to back out, along with a few sprinkles of persuasion trials, that used the words "You shalln't go outside of how the world was meant to go."

Still Amelia responded: "What if the world wasn't meant to go this way in the first place, though?"

Charlie was no match by the enthusiasm spilling out from Amelia's speeches.

There was no stopping them. They had a thought out plan.

Amelia would nod towards Charlie. Charlie would receive it, and would attach to the wheelbarrow heading to give the wheat to the market. Amelia would attach to that same wheelbarrow, on the opposite side, so the delivery man wouldn't notice either side getting heavier.

The both of them would jump off before the wheelbarrow reached the market, and there they would be. On the Underground Railroad.

They tried their plan on their first try, and... it failed.

They were terribly discouraged. Well, Charlie was. Amelia was still excited to carry out their plan.

Amelia was smiling, happy it was so close to working on their first trial! Yet she didn't realize what was happening in the background. Amelia looked over her shoulder when she heard a scream from Charlie.

When the overseer realized they had been on the wheelbarrow, the overseer thought they were trying to poison the crops.

The overseer thought it was entirely Charlie's idea, yet it was entirely Amelia's.

The overseer confronted Charlie. Charlie, confused, responded:

"Who do you see congratulating themselves over something about a wheelbarrow?"

The owner came outside, and told Charlie:

"Don't you talk back to my overseer, you-"

The overseer shouted at Charlie: "You think you can stand up for yourself, eh, Char'? WHO IS THE ONE THAT FORCES YOU TO HARVEST THOSE CROPS?! I AM!! YOU HAVE NO RIGHT TO SPEAK TO ME THAT WAY, CHAR'!!" The owner nodded in agreement.

And the second the overseer got out his whip, Amelia had heard everything. She swiftly looked over only to see the owner holding Charlie into place as the overseer beat him, and beat him, as Charlie screamed as he cried:

"HEEEELP!! HELP ME, ANYONE! PLEASE, STOP, NO!!"

Charlie dropped to the ground, with tears trickling down his face. His arm was broken, blood everywhere, still bleeding, and barely able to move.

Amelia rushed to save her friend, but was taken to the dungeon.

"Oh, come on, you!" The overseer said without hesitance.

"You've seen injuries before!"

Amelia cried while being dragged: "Yes, sir. BUT NOT LIKE THIS!!"

"Oh, shut up, Amelia." Amelia was given a leaf to mouth.

CHAPTER 8

Chapter 8

First time in the dungeon for Amelia was harsh. There was a guy with flies buzzing around him, as he tried to eat them. It disgusted Amelia. Then she discovered why he did it. The guard explained:

"Twerp, don't expect food."

Really?! Amelia thought. She had no idea that the dungeon didn't give out food at all. They could very well starve these poor prisoners to death.

Then, they locked her up, as Amelia stained her clothes with the tears she withdrew from her eyes. Her eyes became clouds as she knocked her back against the cement wall, and slid down.

She thought about how bad Charlie must have been feeling. If they were out of this, every human being in town would help him to a- what is it?- 'hopitall'? Amelia didn't even know what it was.

More droplets rained down her cheeks at the thought of it. No food, no water, nothing to help her or Charlie survive. They could never get on The Underground Railroad.

Sadness overcame her, as she balled up in her little cell.

CHAPTER 9

Chapter 9

Charlie limped across the field, being screamed at by the overseer. After hours and hours of labor, the overseer finally called:

"Break!!"

Everyone grabbed their bottle and chugged, with how thirsty they were. But for Charlie, he instead snuck into the dungeon as the overseer had his lunch break, and slowly tiptoed, disgusted by the man eating flies. At the end of the line, he finally found Amelia.

"Amelia, Amelia! Here you are!" He whispered. Amelia craned her neck sadly. Seeing Charlie with crutches(sticks) in all his pain! She couldn't stand it.

She sniffed, wiped her ears and responded: "What, Charlie? You wanted to acknowledge that I'm terrible by standing up for you and making things worse?"

"Actually, you standing up for me was really kind."

Amelia smiled at the thought that she helped.

They chatted quietly, and then Charlie asked Amelia a very important question.

"Do you want to try and sneak out of this place? After they unlock you out of the dungeon?" Charlie asked.

Amelia smirked at the thought of breaking the rules- for good.

"Of course, Charles.

CHAPTER 10

Chapter 10

Amelia had left the dungeon. Two days of labor in the hot sun without a break! But then, the overseer called:

"Break!!" His raspy voice rang.

It was time for the two escape artists to try their plan again. Every step filled with anxiousness and anticipation, and after the steps were completed, their plan:

Worked.

They were out into the outer world.

They gasped and looked round as the beautiful sun made the sky orange, as it faded into a blue sky. The birds tweeted, adding sound to the slight wind. It was all so romantic, and beyond their wildest dreams, if breaking out of slavery wasn't enough for them. But as they started to head towards town, the owner came up behind them, turning them round by grabbing their shoulders.

"Where are you going?"

Charlie stuttered, but interrupting him the owner responded to nothing:

"Without my help?" Confused, Amelia and Charlie looked at each other.

"I'm trying to have a change of heart. I realize slavery is wrong, so I'm slowly letting go of slaves. But people who like slavery will go after me if they find out I let go of all my slaves."

Charlie and Amelia smiled, and continued.

CHAPTER 11

Chapter 11

They adventured toward town. As they walked they grabbed wild fruit or berries to eat. Three good meals of food a day was a feast to them. They couldn't have a better life now.

But suddenly, Charlie's branch-crutch.. broke!

It snapped in half, and Charlie fell sideways, hitting his broken arm on the ground. The pain was so bad for him he almost fainted when he hit the ground. He had tears and was shouting: "AMELIA!! HELP, PLEASE, PLE.. please.." He didn't have enough breath left in him to continue. But he was conscious, yet he was in *pain*. Then, Amelia found him a new stick.

He grabbed onto it, but had to keep going, no matter how painful it was.

In a few hours, they were there, and saw something they assumed was a signal for slaves, so jumped inside.

CHAPTER 12

Chapter 12

They walked through the door, and there was a woman standing there.

She jumped up in joy and whispered:

"Ah, finally! Slaves!"

Charlie and Amelia were confused. Why was she jumping? Shouldn't she be keeping this secret?

"Ah, that's great! Now I can hand you back to your owner!!" A smile, a smirk, was spreading through her face.

Charlie realized what was happening. He cried: "SLAVE CATCHER!!"

They burst out the door with the woman running after them. Shouting at them to go back to the field, as the two of them answered with a "NO!!" every time.

Finally, they lost her. Then, they found a real station. They entered.

"Hi, I'm Jamie, and I'll be your station master- oh my! We must patch that up, young man! I'll get my first aid kit!"

Charlie and Amelia thought the same thing.

Yep, she's a real station master.

CHAPTER 13

Chapter 13

Charlie felt better then he did as a newborn after being healed due to the bandages given by the incredibly sweet station master.

Amelia couldn't stop thinking about that horrid chase by that slave catcher. The thought of going back to the farm wasn't given any hope. Amelia would do everything to make sure she never went back.

Jamie noticed Amelia's 'sadness' and asked:

"Hey Amelia, what's wrong?"

When Amelia turned around Jamie realized that she was in shock. Charlie explained that they were almost caught by a slave catcher. Jamie remembered she was being chased by a catcher recently as well. But, she mustn't have worried the poor girl, so she replied:

"Oh, Amelia, we should not worry about that, my dear. Whoever tried to catch you is gone now. It's over, little girl, and I shall protect you."

Amelia had a sigh of relief. It was refreshing to know that someone was making sure she and Charlie were safe.

CHAPTER 14

Chapter 14

The 2nd day arised, and the two former slaves woke up for a meal. Jamie was awake at the moment, and had breakfast already served for them in her basement. It was more than a feast for Charlie and Amelia. It was a delicious bacon and eggs meal served to them. They had two courses in one!

Jamie knew they deserved a treat, with all the stories of injustice that entertained her. Charlie and Amelia had quite the lives being the two biggest victims of the injustice. Charlie being weak and Amelia being the only girl on the farm.

Jamie knew she must have to give them the best few weeks of their lives. Charlie and Amelia already were in for it, anyway, but Jamie was just that kind. She wanted to keep it coming.

That lunch they were given a sandwich with various meats. The savory that spread throughout their taste buds was unbelievable!

Dinner was a well cooked chicken, with a salad for whoever preferred it. Charlie headed straight to the heavy meat, while Amelia timidly hulled a fork over to the salad. And oh, was Jamie a cook! Charlie liked the meat even more than the last time, and Amelia loved the collection of timid, yet good flavors from the cucumbers, tomatoes, and lettuce. Lots of healthy, crunchy lettuce!

At the end of the day, the two of them were full. Very full.

CHAPTER 15

Chapter 15

The next day, after the two of them arose, they saw Jamie pull something sharp from her drawer.

"Jamie," Amelia asked, "What is that sharp thing in your drawer?"

"Um, nothing!" Jamie replied.

What actually happened is the slave catcher was back at it, and it was Jamie's job to keep them safe. She was going to try and get rid of the bad guys, but as the kids knocked her to her senses, she realized that it was very cruel and unnecessary.

"What have I done?!" Jamie whispered to herself.

Jamie from that day on felt incredibly terrible and guilty of something she ended up not doing. And it got worse as the children had heavy suspicion of the fact that Jamie may be a slave catcher in disguise.

The two gave awful glances and glares at anything that seemed even fairly suspicious. But, because as the day went on and the two of them never died, they decided to believe Jamie was on their side, and pushed the suspicion away.

Quite the day had happened, but Jamie saw the children lost their glares, and she felt able to fall asleep.

CHAPTER 16

Chapter 16

The sun rose on the fourth day at their first station master's home. Jamie saw everyone was healed and healthy, so she decided today was the day she would prepare them for the next station, where they would go tomorrow.

Jamie packed suitcases with a variety of items which included:

Entertainment, clothing, and books on different lessons. Amelia was given a leather bag, which held everything, and Charlie carried a bag with straps around his arms, and the bag fell against his back.

That day the three ate their meals, and fell asleep, and waited for the next day.

The fifth day appeared, and it was about to be the first day. The two of them grabbed their bags and left, sadly, for Jamie was the best person they had ever met.

Jamie told them this:

"My dearest children, it is time for you to leave. Now, there is a house with a quilt which has a patch with a train sewn on it. Find that house, and there will be a station master. She is close friends with me, so tell her said hi."

The two nodded, and left.

CHAPTER 17

Chapter 17

The two adventured to find the house with a quilt. And after walking around town in their costumes created by Jamie, they found the house.

The quilt was the doormat, and it had colorful patches, with one that was a train. They opened the door, and an older woman brought them downstairs. They went into the pipe room, and that was where they would sleep. But, she had carpeting and lots of colors.

It was a mesmerizing bedroom. They were amazed and knew that this would be a good station.

They unpacked their essentials, and put them in their closet, and put their entertainment and books on a table. It was a good day. The two were full, and asked the master to give them little to eat, but they realized after asking they did not know her name.

"Station Master," Amelia asked in her sweet voice, "What is your name?"

"I go by Martha, sweetheart." She responded.

They nodded, and prepared for a longer station.

CHAPTER 18

Chapter 18

They awoke, and Martha had prepared their breakfast. The pancakes had syrup in the shape of a smile on them, and blueberries as eyes.

Charlie and Amelia were mesmerized by the fact that Martha did this fun idea just for a couple of slaves. They thanked Martha excessively, and Martha took in the appreciation. She enjoyed having slaves stay over. They were so in need and hurt! She loved being able to help others.

Martha gave them a great lunch, with a salad for Amelia, which she had heard about from Jamie, and gave Charlie a healthy, full of protein, entire pound of beef! Martha figured what he didn't eat then would be dinner later.

Amelia loved it! She declared that this salad was her favorite food.

The rest of the afternoon before dinnertime, Charlie and Amelia studied their subjects. They were in their room for a while, and Martha was curious to what was behind their door, so she checked on them.

"Hey guys, what are you up to?" Martha asked.

"Hi Martha! We're practicing our English!" Amelia responded.

"Martha, can you help me?" Charlie asked.

"Yes, Charlie. How can I help you?"

"Well, it says a is pronounced ah, but here a is pronounced ay! I don't understand."

"Well, in English, if there is no consonant after a vowel, then the vowel says what you say when you say the name of the letter, or the long way to say the letter."

"Hm.. I understand. I guess I've been mispronouncing words, and I didn't know."

"Well, mistakes help us learn, my dear."

After dinner, which was a bit late that afternoon due to Charlie's mistake, they went straight to their bed routine.

Charlie thought of that throughout the night. 'Mistakes help us learn.' So true. Like when Amelia and his plan didn't work first, they tried it a bit differently. And, it worked!

"Wow," He whispered to himself. "Such a wise lady."

CHAPTER 19

Chapter 19

That next day, the two slaves awoke to a breakfast of:

A stack of bacon for Charlie, a plate of eggs for Amelia, and pancakes for the both of them.

The two smiled, then dug in. They were given buffets for the first two days, but Martha announced that tomorrow they would be getting healthier meals tomorrow. They knew that Martha would take care of their health, and they trusted her.

As they ate they talked about a variety of ideas, about learning techniques, new meals, bedtime routines, and some possible entertainment.

But, after breakfast, those plans would have to be set aside, for fate had other ideas.

They ate, and were full, and went to their room to read. Martha continued some knitting, but suddenly heard the two

SCREAM.

Martha rushed to their room, only to find their beds empty. Well, almost empty. One of the beds had an envelope in it.

I got your kids
I want $500.00
Give it to me or the kids [illegible]
Deliver the dough to 567 [illegible]
[illegible]

Sincerely,
UNKNOWN

Martha could not let this affect her record. But who has $500 ($500 is now about $12,400.) She had to save them. The kids loved her! She would not leave these poor slaves.

CHAPTER 20

Chapter 20

Charlie and Amelia were fearing this kidnapper much, and Amelia wasn't able to be positive. Where was Martha, and what would become of the two?

The two cried for help in the sound-proof building. Nobody seemed to be coming for them. Charlie and Amelia were both always able to pump each other up, at least, usually Amelia, but it was a very ominous and scary feeling they felt in this situation.

"Amelia," Charlie asked in a shaky voice, due to the fear, "Will we get out of here?"

"I'm not sure, Charles," Amelia responded. "Who would know we are here?"

Charlie gasped. Amelia knew what he was thinking. Tied together, tied to a chair, they had hope. The screamed one thing together:

"MARTHA!!!!"

They screamed so loud that the sound proof barriers couldn't completely hold the sound waves, and Martha barged in.

"Kiddos!" Martha cried. She untied them, and they were about to leave when..

The kidnapper entered.

CHAPTER 21

Chapter 21

"Look who we have here. Some escape artists." The kidnapper said, in a fearful tone. The victims shook, yet Martha stood tall and confident.

"Let them go!" Martha cried.

"Where's my $500?" The kidnapper responded. He was serious about his trade. How would Martha get them out? Unless..

Martha grabbed the kids, and ran for it.

The two watched her, and not only was Martha kind and sweet, they realized she was also brave. This'll be a good station master.

Martha got home, and put them in bed, and gave them the lunch-dinner they deserved. Martha, as she cooked, thought she was a terrible station master for losing them. *I must send them away tomorrow, so they do not have to suffer from my mistakes any more.* She thought.

They ate, went to bed peacefully, and Martha shed tears as she packed their bags.

CHAPTER 22

Chapter 22

Charlie and Amelia awoke, and saw their bags all packed, with Martha standing with a sad smile by their bags.

"Why are these bags full?" Charlie asked.

"Yes, why?" Amelia asked.

"I let you be kidnapped, and I must let you go. I'll be a terrible station master for you." Martha responded.

"No you are not, Martha!" Charlie said.

"Even if I am good sometimes, you cannot overlook how scared I let you be." Martha said. It was too late. She really didn't believe in herself.

The two sadly left, sighing, with their bags in their hands.

"She was such a good station master." Amelia said. Charlie nodded.

"If only she had confidence." Charlie said.

CHAPTER 23

Chapter 23

Charlie and Amelia were clouded with sadness, but they then realized they had no scheduled station master for them! Where would they go?

"Amelia," Charlie said, "Where will we go?" Amelia did not know. But they saw a signal from a little blue house, and they saw it looked familiar.

"Is that.." Charlie said, but Amelia knew what he thought.

"Jamie's house? We can go back!!" Amelia said. The two rushed in, and hugged Jamie.

"Oh, little children! I've missed you very much!" But there was another challenge.

The slave catcher was there. The slave catcher which chased Jamie, the slave catcher who tried to catch the kids, the slave catcher who kidnapped the kids. The slave catcher made them think it was only a hostage, but the slave catcher was behind it all! He had one last trick up his sleeve.

CHAPTER 24

Chapter 24

Jamie put the kids to bed. When she came upstairs.. The door had opened? She closed the door, thinking that it was the wind outside. But Jamie realized the wind was light that night.

Someone came into the house.

Jamie rushed to the kid's room. There was one last note.

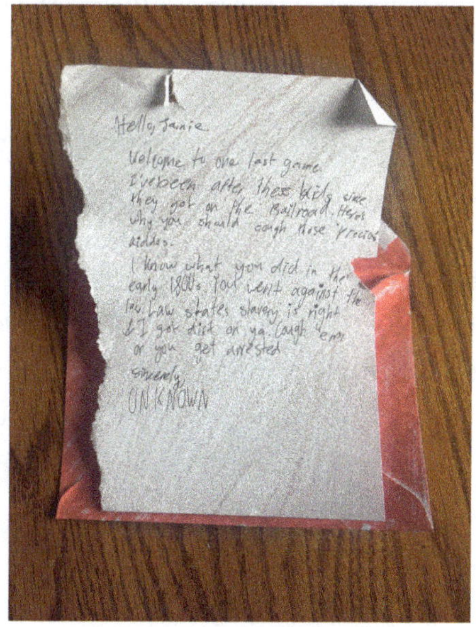

Hello, Jamie

Welcome to one last game.
I've been after these kids since
they got on the Railroad. Here's
why you should caugh those 'precious'
kiddos.
I know what you did in the
early 1800s. You went against the
law. Law states slavery is right
& I got dirt on ya. Caugh 'em
or you get arrested

Sincerely,
UNKNOWN

This was quite the decision. Save these children she has dear to her heart? Or, should she turn them in and feel free of the police? Jamie did not know at the moment. Those kids! But, prison is a lot. Worse than when Jamie was a slave. Then, she made her decision.

The police arrived. The slaves were thrown into her hands.

"Jamie, what do you say?" Said the slave catcher, alongside the officer. The children heard the noise, awoke, and came alongside Jamie. The two were confused about the occurrence. But then, in the midst of the confusion, they heard something very sad, and breathtaking.

"Officer,

arrest me."

Jamie said, as the kids gasped.

Jamie's handcuffs glistened in the moonlight, and the two watched her get shoved in the police's wagon. The tears in the kid's eyes created a fire in their heart, and they would not allow this arrest to take place.

The kids continued to bang on the wagon and yell and scream and scare the horses, to the point where the horses would not gallop. When the officer tried to walk her there the kids blocked the doors. Finally, the officer gave in.

"Alright, alright! Here's Jamie!" Said the officer, declaring their victory and prize, the fact that they had won spun tears again, but this time of happiness. The slave catcher screamed "NOOOoooo!" as the wagon moved away.

In all the excitement, the kids hugged Jamie. The children knew it was a good time. They had been waiting to ask this question.

"Jamie," Amelia said, starting off the question full of love, and then Charlie joined her at the same time, "Will you adopt us?" Jamie smiled and became ever so happy. "Oh, my little ones. Of course!"

And with all the adventures, and that final piece, Charlie, Amelia, and Jamie lived in this lovely house, with a lovely life, forever more, for more adventures in the time.

www.ingramcontent.com/pod-product-compliance
Lightning Source LLC
Chambersburg PA
CBHW070619310726
48982CB00001B/128
* 9 7 9 8 9 9 0 1 5 3 0 0 4 *